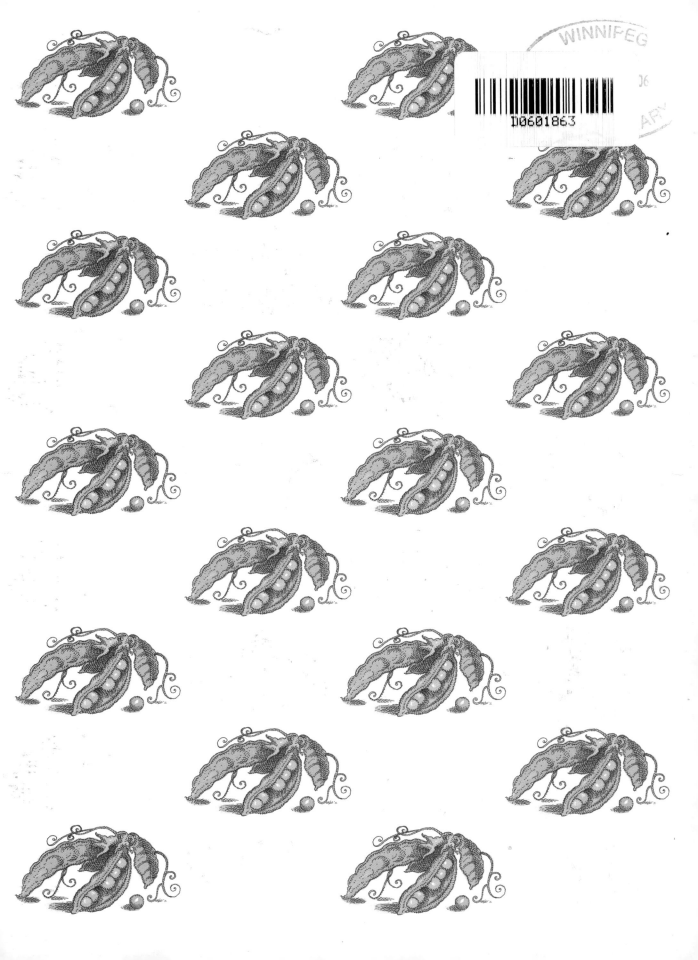

OXFORD
UNIVERSITY PRESS

Great Clarendon Street, Oxford OX2 6DP

Oxford University Press is a department of the University of Oxford.
It furthers the University's objective of excellence in research, scholarship,
and education by publishing worldwide in

Oxford   New York

Auckland Cape Town Dar es Salaam Hong Kong Karachi
Kuala Lumpur Madrid Melbourne Mexico City Nairobi
New Delhi Shanghai Taipei Toronto

With offices in

Argentina Austria Brazil Chile Czech Republic France Greece
Guatemala Hungary Italy Japan Poland Portugal Singapore
South Korea Switzerland Thailand Turkey Ukraine Vietnam

Oxford is a registered trade mark of Oxford University Press
in the UK and in certain other countries

British Library Cataloguing in Publication Data

Data available

ISBN-13: 978-0-19-278237-3 (Hardback)
ISBN-10: 0-19-278237-1 (Hardback)
ISBN-13: 978-0-19-278236-6 (Paperback)
ISBN-10: 0-19-278236-3 (Paperback)
ISBN-13: 978-0-19-275474-5 (Paperback with audio CD)
ISBN-10: 0-19-275474-2 (Paperback with audio CD)

1 3 5 7 9 10 8 6 4 2

Printed in China by Imago

The Princess and the Pea

Ian Beck

OXFORD
UNIVERSITY PRESS

Once upon a time, in a faraway kingdom, there lived a prince. For his twentieth birthday he was given a fine white stallion, called Blaze.

Soon afterwards the king sent for him.

'My boy,' he said, 'it is time you set out and found yourself a real princess to marry.'

So the prince travelled the length and breadth of the world on Blaze. They rode in the summer sun and winter snow, through deserts and over mountains.

The prince met many girls who said that they were princesses. Girls who curtsied very nicely. Girls with eyes hidden behind painted fans. Girls who danced elegantly in bright, silk dresses.

But after all his travels he had never been sure whether any of the girls he had met had been a real princess.

And so, one night, the prince rode back into the palace yard, with his head bowed and a heavy heart. His mother welcomed him back with his favourite meal.

'Come on,' she said. 'Sausages, onion gravy, and mashed potatoes. That ought to cheer you up.'

But even after a hearty supper the prince was still sad. 'I've looked over the whole world, from one end to the other. I'll never find a real princess,' he sighed.

'Don't worry,' said the queen, 'there are ways of telling a real princess. When the right girl comes, I will find out for you, never fear.'

Summer turned to autumn, and great storms shook the kingdom. Hailstones the size of goose eggs crashed around the palace turrets. A great wind tore up the mighty oak tree that the prince had loved since he was a boy.

Winter came, howling in on a blizzard, and the palace was surrounded with deep drifts of snow; even Blaze was kept in the stable under fleecy blankets.

Then one night, the coldest of the year so far, when even the powdered snow had frozen into hard ice, there was a knocking at the palace door. The king was roused from his warm fireside. 'Who on earth can that be out in this awful weather, and at this late hour?' He set off, wrapped in his warmest cloak, and opened the heavy door.

A girl stood knee-deep in a drift of snow. Her fine cape, reduced to rags, was wrapped around her shoulders, and she was huddled and shivering. Her hair was wet around her face, and there were little icicles on her sooty eyelashes.

She fell into the king's arms, and he carried her into the warm parlour. After a few minutes the girl was warmed through. She sat by the fire, drinking a cup of hot chocolate. Some colour had come back into her cheeks, and as she brushed the damp strands of hair away from her face, the prince could see that she might just be beautiful.

The queen glanced at her son and saw that he was gazing at the mysterious girl. 'Tell us about yourself, my dear,' she said.

'I am Princess Phoebe,' said the girl. 'I have been travelling the world, seeking a suitable prince to marry.' She shook her head sadly. 'I have searched for nearly a year with no luck,

for you see he must be a real prince. I was just
on my way home when the blizzard struck.
I stabled my poor horse, and then followed
the lights here.'

The prince was about to speak out when
the queen gestured to him to be quiet.

'You must be exhausted, my dear,' she said
brightly. 'Go and have a hot bath and a good
sleep, and in the morning all shall be well.'

While Phoebe was in her bath, the queen took the prince and two servants to the guest bedchamber. She ordered the servants to strip all the bedding from the bed and take off the mattress. Then the queen took a little silver box from her purse. Inside was a single green pea.

The queen took the pea and placed it on the bed base. Then she ordered the servants

to bring as many mattresses and feather quilts as they could find, and place them all on top of one another. The pile reached almost to the ceiling, and it was a very tall room.

'Now we shall see if she is a real princess,' said the queen. 'Trust me.'

Princess Phoebe spent an uncomfortable night. Despite mattresses, feather quilts, and cosy warmth, things weren't right. No matter how she lay in the bed, no matter how she twisted and turned, she couldn't settle and she didn't sleep a wink.

In the morning, all looked beautiful in the bright sunshine. This would be a fine place to live, Phoebe thought. She went down to the parlour for breakfast.

'Good morning, my dear,' said the queen. 'I hope you slept well.'

Phoebe's eyes had dark circles round them. 'I couldn't sleep at all,' she said. 'No matter how I lay in the bed something was digging into me. I must be covered in bruises.'

It was then that the prince understood. If this girl had felt such a tiny thing as a pea through all those layers of quilts and feathers, then she must be a real princess.

'Look around you, my dear,' said the queen. 'You will see that this is no ordinary house – it is a palace.'

Phoebe looked at all the silverware on the breakfast table, and at the fine silks at the tall windows. At that moment the king entered, with his lord chamberlain.

'If this is a palace,' said Phoebe, 'then you must be the queen, and there, if I am not mistaken, is the king.' At that she curtsied, and then bounced up with a smile on her face. 'Which means that your son is a real prince.'

Later that day the princess's horse was brought from the stables, a fine black mare with a long silky tail. Together the prince and princess set off to ride in the bright winter sunshine.

'Mark my words,' said the queen, 'we'd best set the lord chamberlain to preparing the cathedral for a royal wedding.'

And so they did, and later that year the real prince and the real princess were married, and went to live in their own palace by a lake.

Soon they had to add a nursery, and they all lived happily to the end of their days, which was as long a time as it could be.

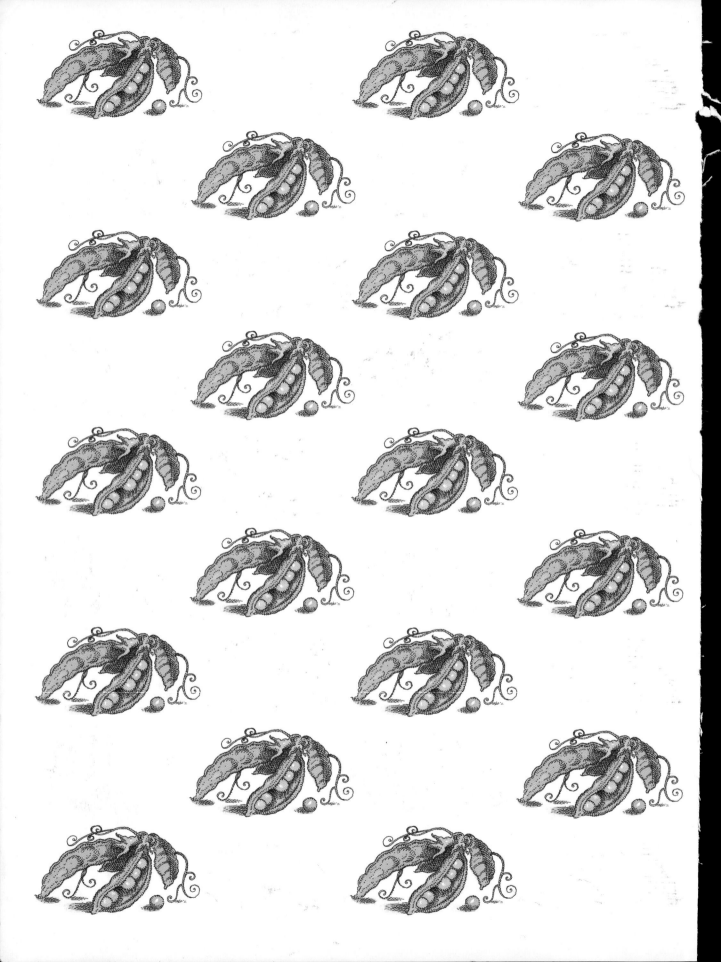